This
Treasure Cove Story
belongs to

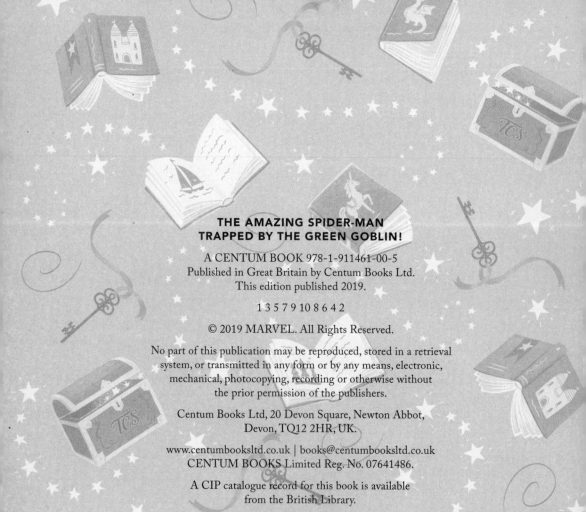

**THE AMAZING SPIDER-MAN
TRAPPED BY THE GREEN GOBLIN!**

A CENTUM BOOK 978-1-911461-00-5
Published in Great Britain by Centum Books Ltd.
This edition published 2019.

1 3 5 7 9 10 8 6 4 2

Centum Books Ltd, 20 Devon Square, Newton Abbot,
Devon, TQ12 2HR, UK.

www.centumbooksltd.co.uk | books@centumbooksltd.co.uk
CENTUM BOOKS Limited Reg. No. 07641486.

A CIP catalogue record for this book is available
from the British Library.

Printed in China.

centum

A Treasure Cove Story

the AMAZING SPIDER-MAN

TRAPPED BY THE GREEN GOBLIN!

Based on the stories by Marvel Comics
By Frank Berrios
Illustrated by Francesco Legramandi and Andrea Cagol

Late one night, the super hero **Spider-Man**
saw some men robbing a warehouse.
'Isn't it a little late to be shopping?'
Spider-Man asked as he swung down on them.

'Spider-Man! Let's get outta here!' yelled one
of the men. He turned to run, but it was too late.
Spider-Man used his **web-shooters** to stop the
thief in his tracks!

Spider-Man followed the thieves into the warehouse.

In the dark building, his **spider-sense** started to tingle – there was danger ahead!

Suddenly, the lights snapped on. It was a trap! The villain known as the **GREEN GOBLIN** laughed.

'All this for me?' Spider-Man joked. 'And it's not even my birthday!'

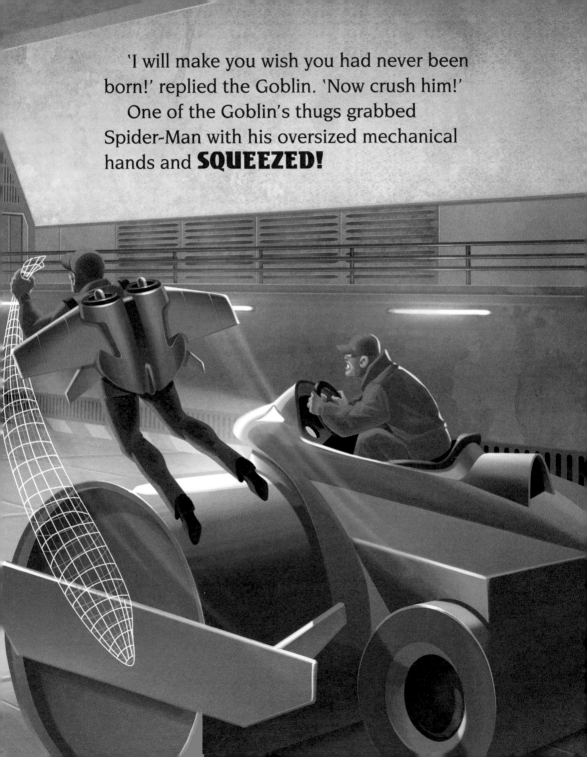

'I will make you wish you had never been born!' replied the Goblin. 'Now crush him!'
   One of the Goblin's thugs grabbed Spider-Man with his oversized mechanical hands and **SQUEEZED!**

'Didn't your mother tell you to keep your hands to yourself?' Spider-Man said, bending the thug's mechanical arms out of shape.

Spider-Man swung through the air. He landed
on the back of a thug wearing a jet pack.
　'Sorry to drop in on you like this,' Spider-Man
said, ripping out the jet pack's wires.

'Happy landings!' said Spider-Man as the thug wearing the jet pack crashed into the oncoming steamroller. **KA-BOOM!**

'Now it's just you and me, Goblin'
said Spider-Man.
'Those fools failed to defeat you,
but I won't,' snarled the Green Goblin.

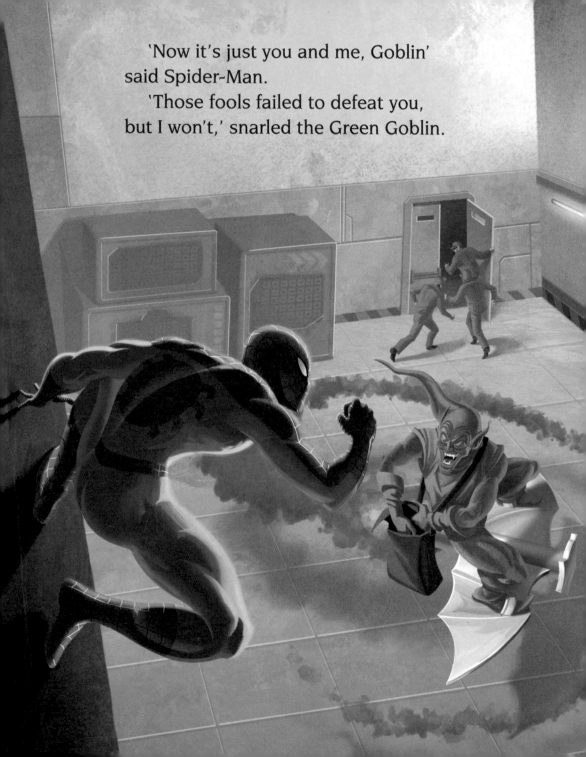

'Take this!' the Green Goblin yelled. He threw a handful of **pumpkin bombs** at Spider-Man. The wall-crawler flipped out of harm's way as the bombs exploded around him.

'Sorry, Goblin – you just don't blow me away!'
said Spider-Man. But suddenly, the Green Goblin
zapped him with a bolt of electricity!

Spider-Man fell into a cage with fast-moving bars. He ducked and dodged the bars, but they were closing in. Soon, he'd be trapped!

'You're the one who belongs behind bars,'
Spider-Man said, 'not me.' With all his strength,
he smashed his way out of the cage!

'Will none of my traps hold you?' the shocked
Green Goblin roared at the wall-crawler.

'You may have escaped, but you will never capture me!' the villain vowed, throwing razor-sharp bat blades as he escaped on his **goblin glider**. 'I will return to destroy you.'

'Do you really think you can beat the one and only Spider-Man with a bunch of high-tech toys?' asked the super hero.

Spider-Man snagged the goblin glider with his web and held on tight. The villain dragged Spider-Man through the air.

'Get off, you annoying insect!' yelled the Goblin. He sent a bolt of electricity through the hero's web.

The Green Goblin laughed and circled back to make sure the hero was done for. Suddenly, the web-slinger moved with incredible speed.

'I'm *shocked* you thought I would fall for that trick again.' Spider-Man used his web-shooters to quickly wrap up the villain from head to toe.

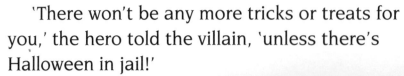

'There won't be any more tricks or treats for you,' the hero told the villain, 'unless there's Halloween in jail!'

Then your friendly neighbourhood Spider-Man swung off in search of his next adventure.

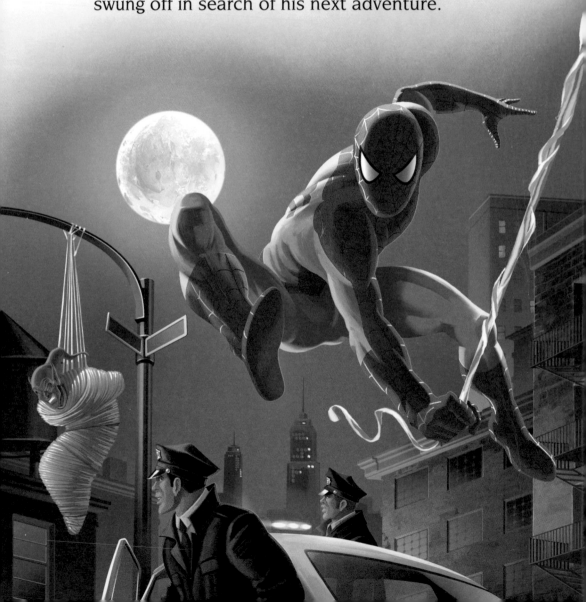

Treasure Cove Stories

*Book list may be subject to change.